The Happy Penguin

Written by Lucy Coult

Illustrated by Anna Jones

Licensed exclusively to Top That Publishing Ltd
Tide Mill Way, Woodbridge, Suffolk, IP12 1AP, UK
www.topthatpublishing.com
Copyright © 2014 Tide Mill Media
All rights reserved
2 4 6 8 9 7 5 3 1
Manufactured in China

Written by Lucy Coult
Illustrated by Anna Jones

ISBN 978-1-78244-949-2

A catalogue record for this book is available from the British Library

The Happy Penguin

Written by Lucy Coult
Illustrated by Anna Jones

On Happy Penguin's last birthday,
his dad was working far away.

His mum bought him a brand new sledge,
and he whizzed it down the icy ledge!

'Yippee!' he cried. He loved his gift,
and laughed as he went through a drift!

Happy Penguin loved to skate,
so he danced upon the frozen lake.

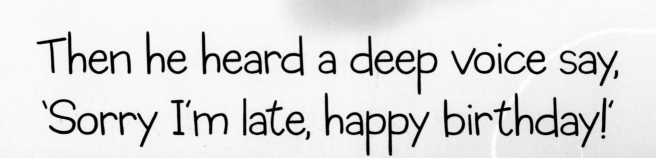

Then he heard a deep voice say,
'Sorry I'm late, happy birthday!'

It was Happy Penguin's dad!
And now he was so very glad.

His mum had made a lovely dish,
a birthday cake made out of fish!

Now they were at home together,
it was Happy Penguin's best birthday ever!

The End

The Little Seal

Written by Lucy Coult
Illustrated by Anna Jones

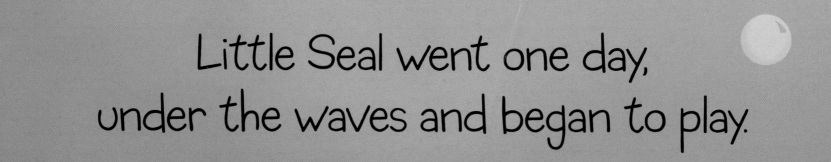

Little Seal went one day,
under the waves and began to play.

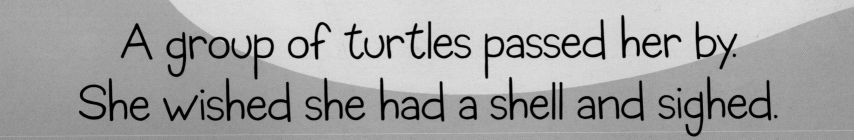

A group of turtles passed her by.
She wished she had a shell and sighed.

She scared a squid, and began to think,
how fun it would be to squirt some ink!

A crab crawled sideways to the shore.
She saw it move and loved its claws.

Something tickled Little Seal's tummy.
She turned and laughed, it was her mummy!

Her mum told her she had no flaws,
for seals don't need shells, ink or claws!

Little Seal has different features,
but she's just as good as other creatures.

Her mum thinks she's perfect as can be,
and now Little Seal swims happily!

The End

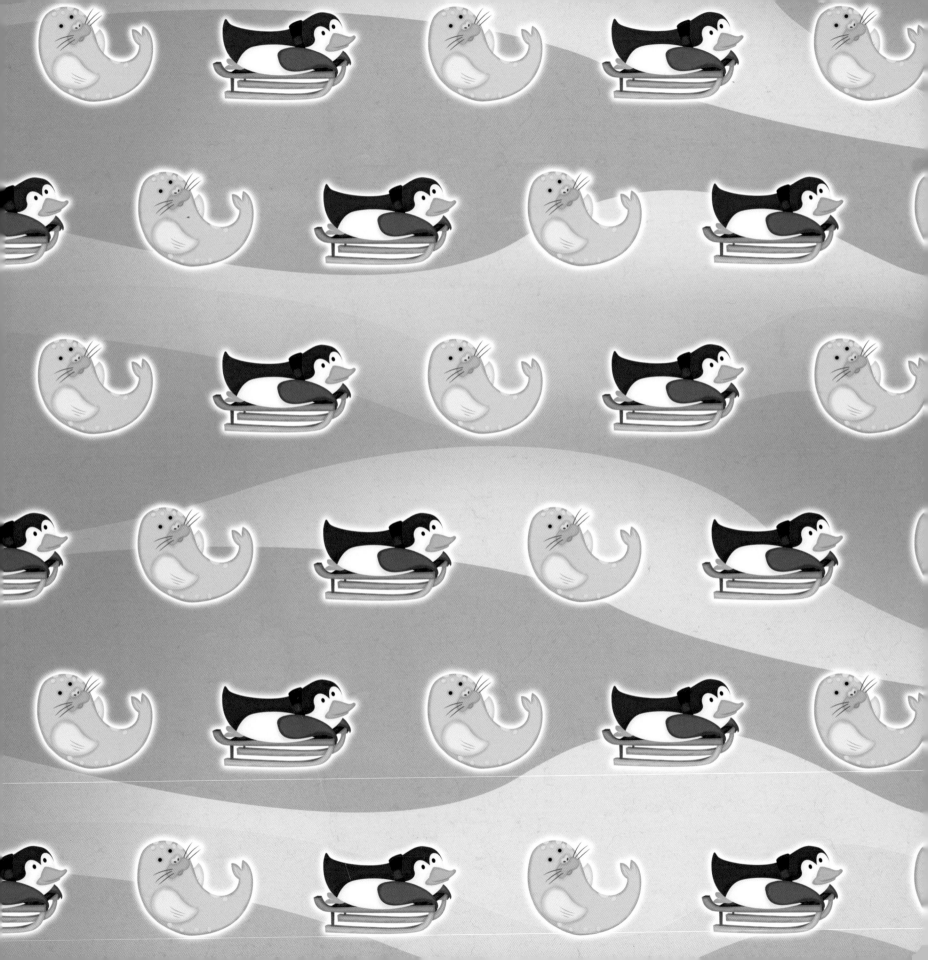

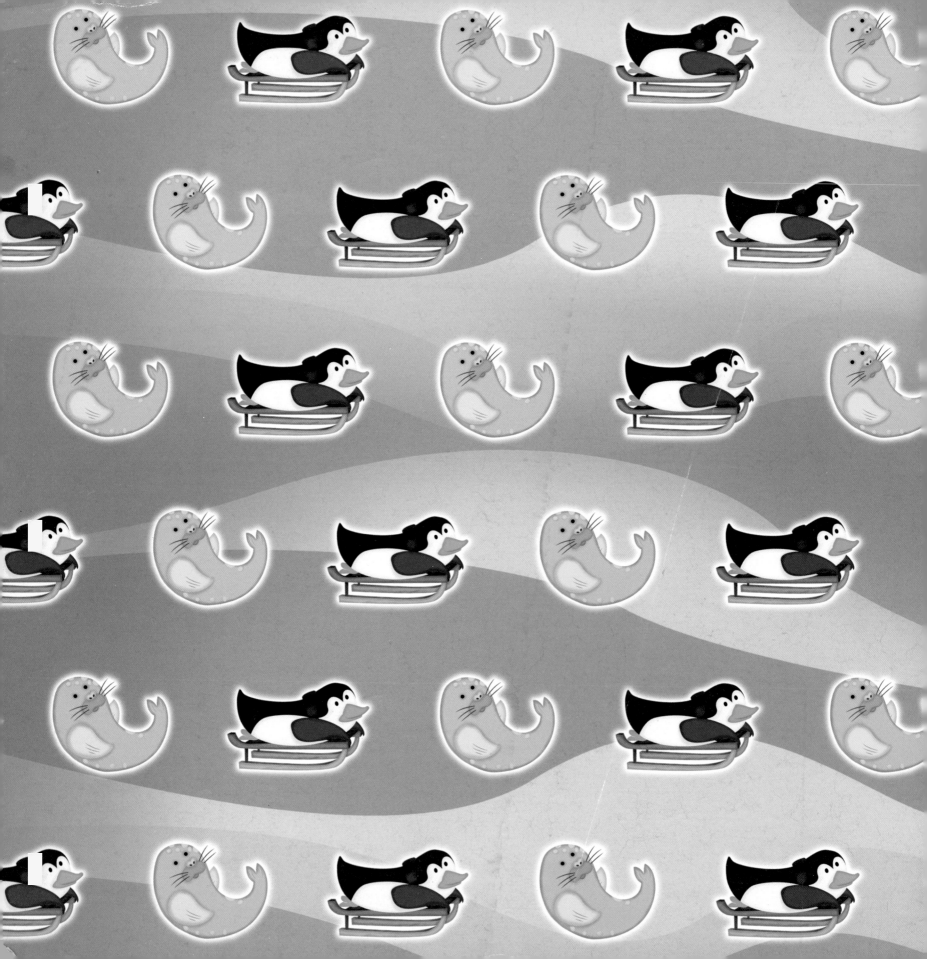